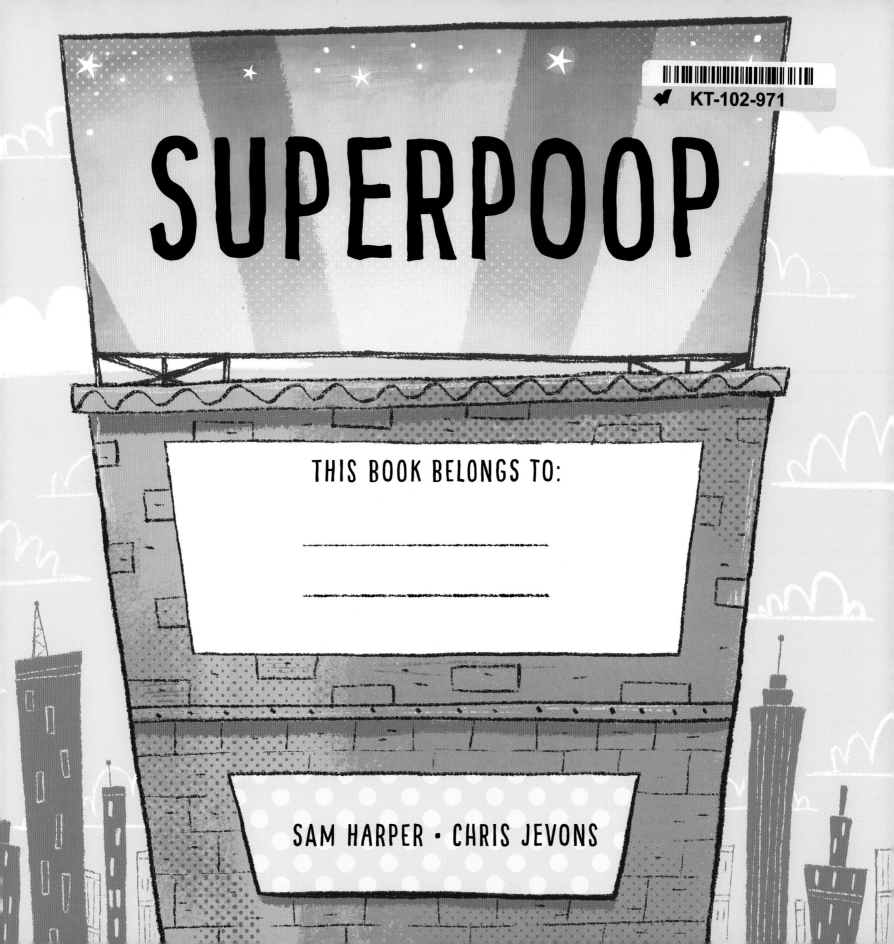

SUPERPOOP

THIS BOOK BELONGS TO:

_____

_____

SAM HARPER · CHRIS JEVONS

FOR STEWART AND JAMES, MY NUMBER TWO FANS!
S.H.

FOR CHESTER
C.J.

HODDER CHILDREN'S BOOKS
First published in Great Britain in 2021 by Hodder and Stoughton
3 5 7 9 10 8 6 4
© Hachette Children's Books, 2021
Illustrated by Chris Jevons

ISBN 978 1 44495 686 3

Printed in China

Hodder Children's Books
An imprint of Hachette Children's Group
Part of Hodder and Stoughton
Carmelite House, 50 Victoria Embankment
London, EC4Y 0DZ
An Hachette UK Company
www.hachette.co.uk
www.hachettechildrens.co.uk

SUPERPOOP

Hodder
Children's
Books

Meet SUPERPOOP!

He's your friendly local **POOPERHERO** in training! Superpoop just needs to perform one **TOOT**-ally amazing rescue to earn his place in the Super League of Superheroes.

Will anyone send out a call for help?

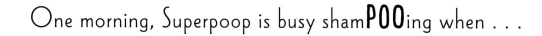

One morning, Superpoop is busy shamPOOing when . . .

RING-RING! RING-RING!

"My first call on the **POO**phone!" Superpoop shouts.

"Hello, how may I help **POO**?

There's a large **MESS** floating in the pool, you say?

I'm on my way. Superpoop to the rescue!"

Superpoop makes a big splash at the Wacky Waves Waterpark.
"Have no fear! I'm here to **WIPE UP** the mess!
Now, where's that **FLOATER?**"

"Got you!" says the lifeguard.

"But **I'VE** come to save **YOU!**" cries Superpoop, looking flushed.

"No need!" shouts Octogirl,
sliding onto the scene.
"I'll untangle this **MESS**
in no time!"

"Oh **PLOP**," sighs Superpoop.
"I guess this isn't the job for me."

Later that day, Superpoop is ironing his superpants when . . .

RING-RING! RING-RING!

SUPERPOOP SEARCH

"Job number two! A **POWERFUL BLAST** at your party, you say? This one is definitely a job for Superpoop!"

"PLOPS AWAAAAAAY!"

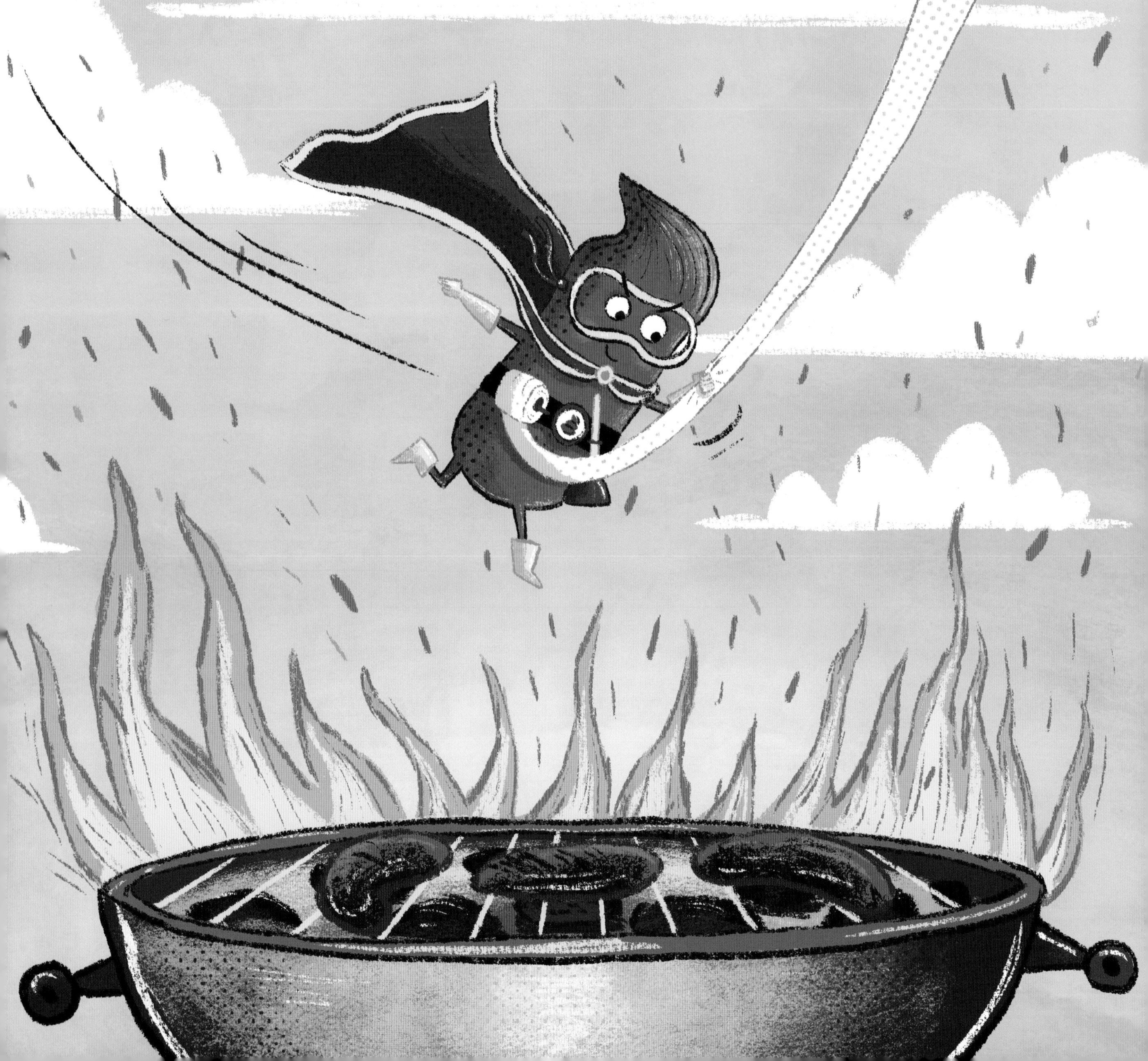

Superpoop crash-lands into the barbecue party.

"I'm here to save you from the **SMELLY BLAST!**" he yells. "Hmm, I don't smell any parps . . ."

"Don't be a party **POOPER**, Superpoop.
I've got it covered!" calls Wonderduck.

SPLASH!

"You've got to be **SKIDDING** me," sighs Superpoop.

"When will I find a job that's right for me?"

Every time the **POO**phone rings, Superpoop leaps into action.
But every time, another hero takes care of business.

Superpoop is even beaten by Safety Stan
to help old Mrs Peck cross the road!

"For **POOP'S** sake, how will I ever prove I'm more than just a **PLOP?**"
Superpoop is ready to give up when . . . **"HELP!"**

Following the cry, Superpoop skids round the corner.
At the museum, he finds the guard in a terrible flap.

"WHAT'S THE PROBLEM HERE?"

Superpoop asks in his biggest, boldest superhero voice.

"Crooked Croc has stolen the museum's most precious diamond!" says Octogirl. "He's escaped down the drain and sealed it off. We don't know what to do."

"Toilet trouble? Now **THAT** sounds like a job for Superpoop!"

Superpoop spies Crooked Croc in the sewer ahead.

"Stop right there, thief! I'm here to bring you to justice!"

Crooked Croc turns in surprise. "And just *who* are *you*?" he scoffs.

"Me?" smiles the daring pooperhero. "I'm the **NEW SKID** on the block . . .

... I'M SUPERPOOP!

He ducks and rolls –
SLOOSH!

Crooked Croc slips and falls.

POW!

Superpoop grabs Croc,
and with mighty concentration . . .

PARP!

"You saved the day, Superpoop!" shouts Octogirl.

"We could use a hero like you in the Super League,"
Giganta-raffe says.

"Three cheers for Superpoop!" they all yell.
"HIP-HIP-POO-RAY! HIP-HIP-POO-RAY!
HIP-HIP-POO-RAY!"

DIAMOND

If you're causing toilet trouble, he'll flush you down.

And thanks to his special set of skills . . .

. . . he is never late when nature calls.

"PLOPS AWAY!"